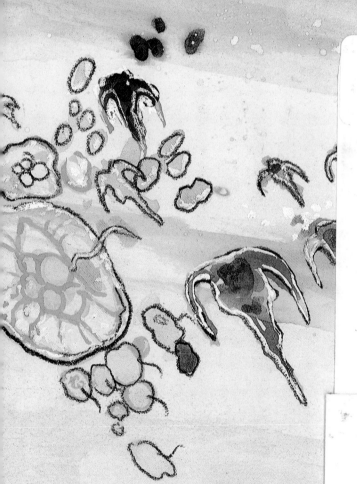

This is
the Sea
that Feeds Us

To my grandson, Harper—*RFB*

To Susan, who has always been there for me, just in a different time zone.—*DD*

Copyright © 1998 Robert F. Baldwin
Illustrations copyright © 1998 Don Dyen

Baldwin, Robert F.
    This is the sea that feeds us / by Robert F. Baldwin; illustrated
by Don Dyen—1st ed.
    p. cm.
    Summary: This cumulative rhyme portrays the ocean's
intricate food web, with each verse introducing another hungry
creature, from the tiny plankton up to a grateful family of humans.
    ISBN 1-883220-69-6 (hardcover)
    ISBN 1-883220-70-X (paper)
    [1. Food chains (Ecology)-Fiction. 2. Marine ecology-Fiction.
3. Ecology-fiction. 4. Stories in rhyme.] I. Dyen, Don, ill.
    II. Title.

PZ8.3.B18Th   1998 [E]-dc21
                                                97-42916

Published by DAWN Publications
P.O. Box 2010
Nevada City, CA 95959
530-478-0111

Email: inquiries@DawnPub.com
Website: www.DawnPub.com

Printed in China

10 9 8 7 6 5 4 3
First Edition

Designed by Brook Design Group

This is the Sea that Feeds Us

By Robert F. Baldwin • Illustrated by Don Dyen

DAWN PUBLICATIONS

This is the sea that feeds us.

This is the sun
that shines on the sea that feeds us.

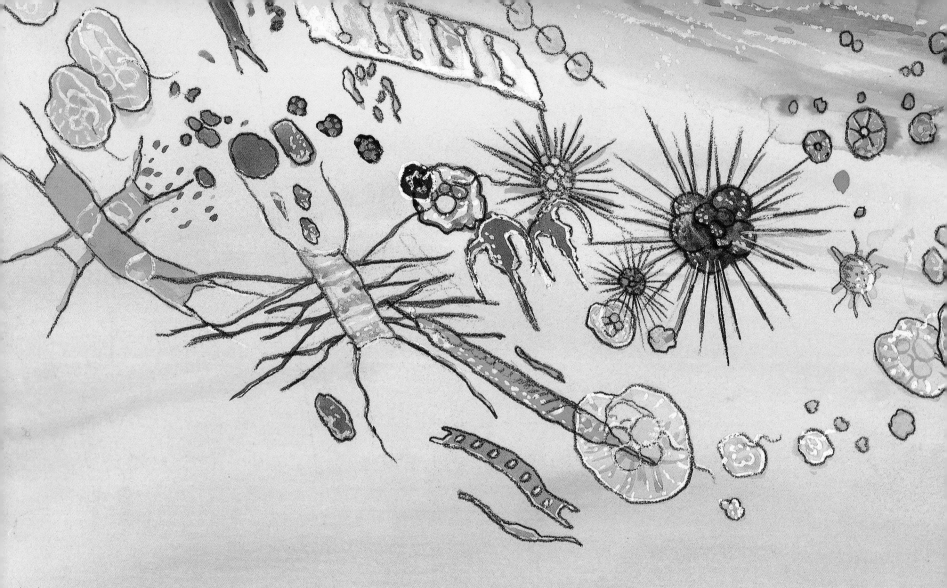

These are the plankton, floating free,
zillions of creatures alive in the sea,
making their food from the light of the sun
that shines on the sea that feeds us.

THESE ARE PHYTOPLANKTON.
"Phyto" means plant and "plankton" means wandering.
Phytoplankton are wandering plants.

Here is a shrimp, as small as a snail
(lots of legs and a squiggly tail)
dining on plankton, floating free,
zillions of creatures alive in the sea,
making their food from the light of the sun
that shines on the sea that feeds us.

VERY YOUNG SHRIMP EAT PHYTOPLANKTON,
but as they get bigger they eat zooplankton,
a tiny animal that eats phytoplankton.

A curious girl with a sandy pail
caught a shrimp as small as a snail
(lots of legs and a squiggly tail)
that ate the plankton, floating free,
zillions of creatures alive in the sea,
making their food from the light of the sun
that shines on the sea that feeds us.

NOTHING WOULD LIVE IN THE OCEANS
if there were no phytoplankton.
They are like "ocean grass" —
the basic food of the sea.

This is the wind, mighty and grand,
that drove the waves upon the sand
and made the gloomy storm clouds fly
like airborne whales across the sky.

The roaring wind and the booming gale
thrilled the girl with the sandy pail
who caught the shrimp as small as a snail
(lots of legs and a squiggly tail)
that ate the plankton, floating free,
zillions of creatures alive in the sea,
making their food from the light of the sun
that shines on the sea that feeds us.

STORMS AND STRONG CURRENTS HELP
PHYTOPLANKTON TO GROW *by churning*
up nutrients from deeper down in the ocean.

A mother stood by the sandy shore,
watching the ocean tumble and roar.
She hugged the girl with the sandy pail
and baited a hook in the blustery gale
with a little shrimp as small as a snail
(lots of legs and a squiggly tail)
that ate the plankton, floating free,
zillions of creatures alive in the sea,
making their food from the light of the sun
that shines on the sea that feeds us.

FISH LIKE THIS BLACK SEA BASS eat shrimp or smaller fish,
which eat zooplankton, which eat phytoplankton.

This is the fish with a hungry look
that saw the shrimp, but not the hook
as the mother fished in the booming gale
that thrilled the girl with the sandy pail
who caught the shrimp as small as a snail
(lots of legs and a squiggly tail)
that ate the plankton, floating free,
zillions of creatures alive in the sea,
making their food from the light of the sun
that shines on the sea that feeds us.

And when the wind had gone its way,
and the fiddler crabs came out to play,
a barefoot man, all jolly and brown
built a fire as the sun went down.

The people, as they began to cook,
thanked the fish with the hungry look.
They thanked the sea that feeds us all,
that feeds the creatures great and small;

that feeds the crabs, and feeds the whales,
and feeds the sharks, and feeds the snails,
and feeds the ocean's fabulous fishes
a feast of their favorite seafood dishes,
and feeds each shrimp, as small as a snail
(lots of legs and a squiggly tail)
a supper of plankton, floating free,
zillions of creatures alive in the sea,

THE OCEAN NOT ONLY GIVES FOOD,
it gives oxygen too. Phytoplankton produce
more than half the world's oxygen supply.

making their food from the light of the sun
and gone with the tide when the day is done,
adrift in the sea that feeds us.

YOU CANNOT SEE THEM WITHOUT A MICROSCOPE,
but millions of phytoplankton may live in one quart of seawater—
the silent, invisible basis of life in the sea.

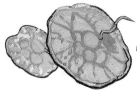# THE MAGIC OF HOW THE SEA FEEDS US

THE SMALLEST CREATURES IN THE OCEAN are the real heroes of this story. They are the phytoplankton, tiny plants which have been living in the ocean for about 300 million years. There are thousands of different kinds of them. They come in many shapes and designs, and are all so small that you cannot see them except through a microscope. Even if you put five million of these single-celled plants together, they would form a greenish glob about the size of a pea! Yet all the creatures of the sea depend on them for food.

PHYTOPLANKTON DON'T HAVE TO EAT ANYTHING to live—like many other plants, they simply create their own food from sunlight in a magical process called "photosynthesis." A very special greenish substance in each phytoplankton, called chlorophyll, enables them to turn the energy of the sun into sugar and oxygen.

THIS SUGAR GIVES THEM THE ENERGY THEY NEED to reproduce, which they do just about every day. Each cell simply divides itself in half and then there are two. Going from one to two may not seem like a fast way to grow, but just figure it out—if a single phytoplankton and its "children" divide themselves every day, there would be 1,048,576 phytoplankton in only 20 days! Phytoplankton produce more plant growth than all plants growing on land put together.

AT THAT RATE, THE OCEANS OF THE WORLD would soon become a gooey green mess of phytoplankton. That doesn't happen because other sea creatures, including clams, oysters, barnacles, sea urchins, sea worms and baby shrimp eat phytoplankton by the millions. Then other bigger creatures—such as fish, lobsters, seals, sharks, whales and birds—eat the smaller creatures. All plants and animals that live in the sea are part of what is called the "marine food web." Each creature except phytoplankton depends on the web for food, and all of them—especially the phytoplankton—give food to the web.

NOT ONLY DO ALL SEA CREATURES DEPEND ON PHYTOPLANKTON for food, but humans and every animal that breathes also depend on phytoplankton, because of the oxygen they make. The zillions of phytoplankton alive in the world's oceans make more oxygen, even, than all the trees and plants that grow on land put together. In fact, long before trees or plants grew on Earth, the Earth's atmosphere was being formed from the oxygen created by phytoplankton.

OUR LIVES ARE CONNECTED, more than we may realize, to the watery part of our world. If people protect the oceans and keep them healthy, the phytoplankton and the sea will continue to produce food and oxygen for as long as the sun shines.

ABOUT THE AUTHOR AND ILLUSTRATOR

Robert F. Baldwin, of Newcastle, Maine and Des Moines, Iowa has spent much of his life on or near the ocean. His articles and stories about the sea, the people who work on it, and the creatures that live in it have appeared in such magazines as *Sea Frontiers, Down East, Offshore and Yankee.* His first book for children, *New England Whaler,* was published in 1996 by Lerner Publications.

Don Dyen likes to fish, although he prefers to let someone else bait the hook. When it comes to painting, however, he doesn't mind getting his hands messy. He is an experienced illustrator, especially of textbooks and children's books. This is the first portrait that he has done of a shrimp. He lives in Bucks County, Pennsylvania.

OTHER DISTINCTIVE NATURE AWARENESS BOOKS FROM DAWN PUBLICATIONS

A Drop Around the World, by Barbara Shaw McKinney, follows a single drop of water—from snow to steam, from polluted to purified, from stratus cloud to subterranean crack. Drop inspires our respect for water's unique role on Earth. (Teacher's Guide available.)

A Swim through the Sea, by Kristin Joy Pratt, uses delightful alliterative verse and alphabet book format to introduce the ocean habitat. (Teacher's Guide available.)

Seashells by the Seashore, by Marianne Berkes, introduces young children to little sea creatures that build their shell homes in a wonderful variety of shapes and colors. In this engaging rhyme, children comb the beach, counting, collecting and naming beautiful shells.

The Dandelion Seed, by Joseph Anthony, uses stunning illustrations and a simple but profound parable to tell of a seed's journey through the world—a journey of challenge as well as wonder and beauty.

Places of Power, by Michael DeMunn, reveals what native people have always known: Earth has places of power that speak to the open heart. DeMunn gives authentic instruction to children and adults alike in how to find that place.

Lifetimes, by David Rice, introduces some of nature's longest, shortest, and most unusual lifetimes, and what they have to teach us. This book teaches, but it also goes right to the heart. (Teacher's Guide available.)

DAWN publications is dedicated to inspiring in children a deeper understanding and appreciation for all life on Earth. For a copy of our catalog please call 800-545-7475. Please also visit our web site at www.dawnpub.com.

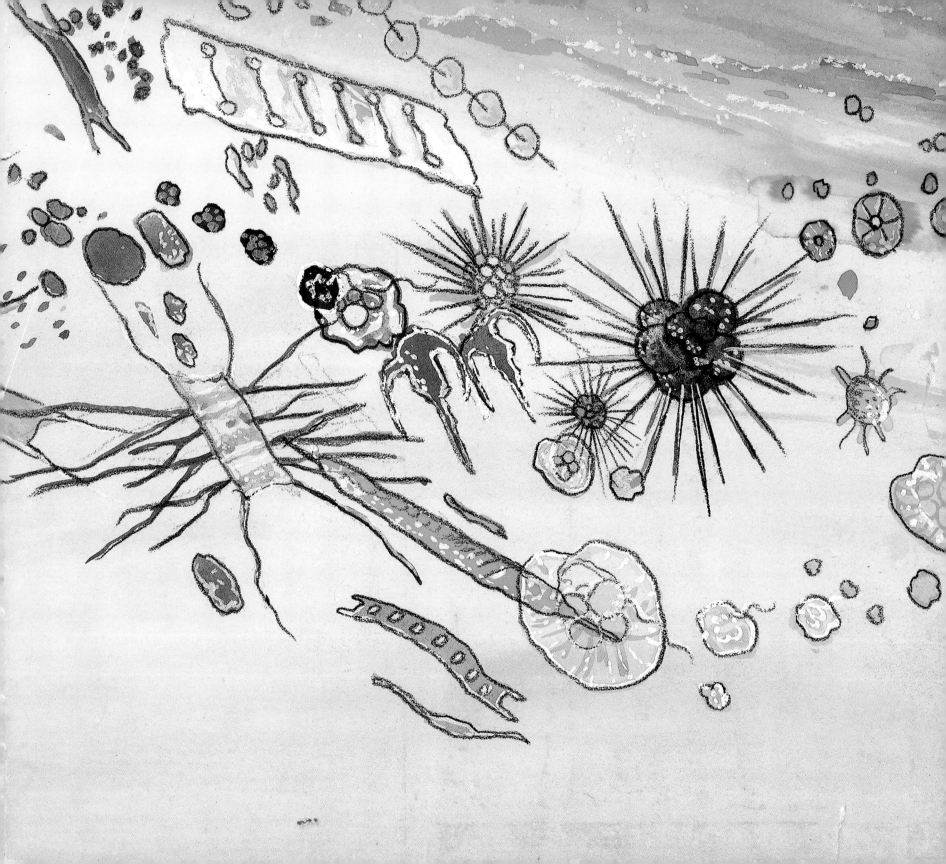